Ladybird I'm Ready...
for Phonics!

Note to parents, carers and teachers

Ladybird I'm Ready for Phonics is a series of phonic reading books that have been carefully written to give gradual, structured practice of the synthetic phonics programme your child is learning at school.

Each book focuses on a set of phonemes (sounds) together with their graphemes (letters). The books also provide practice of common tricky words, such as **the** and **said**, that cannot be sounded out.

The series closely follows the order that your child is taught phonics in school, from initial letter sounds to key phonemes and beyond. It helps to build reading confidence through practice of these phonics building blocks, and reinforces school learning in a fun way.

Ideas for use

- Children learn best when reading is a fun experience. Read the book together and give your child plenty of praise and encouragement.

- Help your child identify and sound out the phonemes (sounds) in any words he is having difficulty reading. Then, blend these sounds together to read the word.

- Talk about the story words and tricky words at the end of each story to reinforce learning.

For more information and advice on synthetic phonics and school book banding, visit **www.ladybird.com/phonics**

Book Band 3

Level 8 builds on the sounds learnt in levels 1 to 7
and introduces new sounds and their letter representations:

ar   or   ur   ow   oi   er

Special features:

repetition of sounds
in different words

short sentences with
simple language

Now, Carl has to sell the corn in town. He loads up his cart.

Carl's sister pops on her coat. Will she go and join him?

Yes, the town shops are good.

24

25

Story Words

Can you match these words to the pictures below?

farmer

sister

corn

town

book

coat

Tricky Words

These tricky words are in the story you have just read. They cannot be phonetically sounded out. Can you memorize them and read them super fast?

into	her
the	he
go	she
no	are
my	all
to	

30

31

summary page to
reinforce learning

Written by Monica Hughes
Illustrated by Chris Jevons

Phonics and Book Banding Consultant: Kate Ruttle

A catalogue record for this book is available from the British Library

Published by Ladybird Books Ltd
80 Strand, London, WC2R 0RL
A Penguin Company

001

ISBN: 978-0-72327-544-2
Printed in China

Ladybird I'm Ready... for Phonics!

Martin and Roberta

Martin and Roberta
are farmers.

Martin has a turnip farm and Roberta has a leek farm.

A turnip fit for a king.

A leek fit for a queen.

Martin joins Roberta on the road to town.

It is wet, wet, wet!

Town →

Martin bows to the king.

This turnip is all for you!

Roberta tells the queen the leek is all for her.

Roberta and Martin go off
for a chat.

The butler tells Martin and Roberta they can now join the king and queen.

This turnip is for the queen!

This leek is for the king!

The king and queen had
turnip and leek for supper.

Story Words

Can you match these words
to the pictures below?

leek

turnip

king

queen

butler

Martin

Roberta

Tricky Words

These tricky words are in the story you have just read. They cannot be phonetically sounded out. Can you memorize them and read them super fast?

are

the

to

go

they

me

you

her

all

Ladybird I'm Ready...
for Phonics!

Farmer Carl

Farmer Carl has to pop the seeds into the soil.

Will his sister go and join him? No!

Carl pops in all the seeds.

The corn gets taller and taller.

Carl has to cut it down.

Will his sister go and join him now? No!

Ow, my back hurts.

Carl cuts down all the corn.

Now, Carl has to sell the corn in town. He loads up his cart.

Carl's sister pops on her coat.
Will she go and join him?

Did Carl let her go to town?
No! She did not help.
She can not go to town.

Carl sells all his corn.

Then, Carl gets a book.

Story Words

Can you match these words
to the pictures below?

farmer

sister

corn

town

book

coat

Tricky Words

These tricky words are in the story you have just read. They cannot be phonetically sounded out. Can you memorize them and read them super fast?

into   her

the   he

go   she

no   are

my   all

to

Collect all
Ladybird I'm Ready...
for Phonics!

Captain Comet's Space Party — 9780723275374

Nat Naps! — 9780723275381

Top Dog — 9780723275398

Huff! Puff! Run! — 9780723275404

Fix It Vets — 9780723275411

Dash is Fab! — 9780723275428

Big, Big Fish — 9780723275435

Dig, Farmer, Dig! — 9780723275442

Fun Fair Fun — 9780723275459

Wow, Wowzer! — 9780723275466

Wizard Woody — 9780723275473

Monster Stars — 9780723275480

Say the Sounds — 9780723271598

Flashcards — 9780723272069